10

THINGS I LOVE
ABOUT
DINOSAURS

by
Samantha Sweeney

Illustrated by
Rob McClurkan

tiger tales

The **NUMBER ONE** thing I love about dinosaurs is KNOWING THEIR NAMES. I know at least 20 and practice all the long words. My dad only knows three! He says I'm an "Expert-osaurus."

DINO ZONE

My favorite name is *Pterodactyl* (even though they're not official dinosaurs, they're prehistoric flying reptiles) because it has a silent "p." And it reminds me of my favorite joke!

What is the scariest prehistoric creature? A Terror—dactyl!

DINO EXPERT

I'm really good at testing Dad's dinosaur knowledge because . . .

The **NUMBER TWO** thing I love about dinosaurs is READING ABOUT THEM IN BOOKS. The library has so many great books with awesome pictures and amazing facts. Like, did you know that the first dinosaurs lived on Earth almost 250 million years ago?

I tried to figure out how many times my own age that is, but there aren't enough zeros in the world!

AMAZING DINOSAURS

FOSSILS

DINOSAURS OF THE TRIASSIC PERIOD

I'm learning SO much about dinosaurs, like . . .

The **NUMBER THREE**
thing I love about dinosaurs is that
SOME LEARNED TO FLY! They had
feathers and wings—just like
birds. Scientists say that
birds today are related to
ancient dinosaurs!

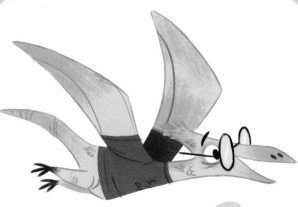

I wish I could
fly, too!

I love to fill my brain with exciting
dinosaur facts, and . . .

The **NUMBER FOUR** thing I love about dinosaurs is learning WHAT THEY ATE. I know about *herbivores*—the dinosaurs that only ate plants—and *carnivores*, the dinosaurs that only ate meat.

An herbivore is a vegetarian—just like Aunt Sophie!

Hey, Carnivore, stay away from my dinner!

Some dinosaurs are scary, but . . .

The **NUMBER FIVE**
thing I love about dinosaurs is that
THE BIG ONES DIDN'T ALWAYS WIN!
When we set up races in our bedroom,
my older brother always gets to be the
T. rex—they could be 40 feet long and
weigh more than 7 tons!

The **NUMBER SIX** thing I love about dinosaurs is when my little sister has a DINOSAUR-THEMED PARTY. All her friends dress up in cute costumes, they eat fun party food like dino bones (they're really pretzels) and dino eggs (they're grapes), and Mom makes a cool volcano cake.

The **NUMBER SEVEN** thing I love about dinosaurs is A TRIP TO THE DINOSAUR MUSEUM! My most favorite thing is going to see the *Diplodocus* skeleton. You can get right up close and see how **ENORMOUS** it was—about 175 feet long. That's almost half a football field!

I get a special badge that says "I'm a young explorer."
Exploring is SO fun, and that's why . . .

The **NUMBER EIGHT** thing I love about dinosaurs is FOSSIL HUNTS. We go on expeditions, and *paleontologists* help us dig carefully for bones or fossilized shells or footprints. A paleontologist is someone who studies *fossils* to understand more about the history of life on Earth. How cool is that?

Maybe one day I'll discover a new species of dinosaur that would be named after me!

When I get home, it's time for . . .

The **NUMBER NINE** thing I love about dinosaurs—
BUILDING VOLCANOES! I use baking soda to make the volcano
erupt, and Mom says it's really a mini science class because
I'm doing an experiment.

I do really LOUD explosion noises, and . . .

The **NUMBER TEN** thing I love about dinosaurs is PRACTICING MY ROAR! Sometimes, we all sit on the couch, put on our favorite dinosaur movie, and take turns making all the noises.

Scientists think that's how dinosaurs communicated. Some of them had very small brains, so maybe a grunt was all they could manage!

It would be kind of scary to hear a real dinosaur roar. But then I realize that the thing I love most about dinosaurs is . . .

. . . they are extinct,
so they'll never catch me!